# OVER THE MOON

## A COLLECTION OF FIRST BOOKS

*Goodnight Moon, The Runaway Bunny,* and *My World*

by **Margaret Wise Brown**

Pictures by **Clement Hurd**

✎ **HARPERCOLLINS** *PUBLISHERS*

# GOODNIGHT MOON

by Margaret Wise Brown
Pictures by Clement Hurd

# GOODNIGHT MOON

by Margaret Wise Brown
Pictures by Clement Hurd

In the great green room
There was a telephone
And a red balloon
And a picture of—

**The cow jumping over the moon**

**And there were three little bears sitting on chairs**

And two little kittens
And a pair of mittens

And a little toyhouse
And a young mouse

**And a comb and a brush and a bowl full of mush**

**And a quiet old lady who was whispering "hush"**

Goodnight room

**Goodnight moon**

**Goodnight cow jumping over the moon**

**Goodnight light**
**And the red balloon**

**Goodnight bears**
**Goodnight chairs**

**Goodnight kittens**

**And goodnight mittens**

Goodnight clocks
And goodnight socks

Goodnight little house

And goodnight mouse

Goodnight comb
And goodnight brush

Goodnight nobody

**Goodnight mush**

And goodnight to the old lady
whispering "hush"

**Goodnight stars**

**Goodnight air**

Goodnight noises everywhere

# The RUNAWAY BUNNY

by Margaret Wise Brown
Pictures by Clement Hurd

# THE
# RUNAWAY BUNNY

## by Margaret Wise Brown
## Pictures by Clement Hurd

HarperCollins*Publishers*

Once there was a little bunny who wanted to run away.
So he said to his mother, "I am running away."
"If you run away," said his mother, "I will run after you.
For you are my little bunny."

"If you run after me," said the little bunny,
"I will become a fish in a trout stream
and I will swim away from you."

"If you become a fish in a trout stream," said his mother,
"I will become a fisherman and I will fish for you."

"If you become a fisherman," said the little bunny,
"I will become a rock on the mountain, high above you."

"If you become a rock on the mountain high above me,"
said his mother, "I will be a mountain climber,
and I will climb to where you are."

"If you become a mountain climber,"
said the little bunny,
"I will be a crocus in a hidden garden."

"If you become a crocus in a hidden garden,"
said his mother, "I will be a gardener. And I will find you."

"If you are a gardener and find me,"
said the little bunny, "I will be a bird
and fly away from you."

"If you become a bird and fly away from me,"
said his mother, "I will be a tree that you come home to."

"If you become a tree," said the little bunny,
"I will become a little sailboat,
and I will sail away from you."

"If you become a sailboat and sail away from me,"
said his mother, "I will become the wind
and blow you where I want you to go."

"If you become the wind and blow me," said the little bunny,
"I will join a circus and fly away on a flying trapeze."

"If you go flying on a flying trapeze," said his mother,
"I will be a tightrope walker,
and I will walk across the air to you."

"If you become a tightrope walker and walk across the air,"
said the bunny, "I will become a little boy
and run into a house."

"If you become a little boy and run into a house,"
said the mother bunny, "I will become your mother
and catch you in my arms and hug you."

"Shucks," said the bunny, "I might just as well
stay where I am and be your little bunny."

And so he did.

"Have a carrot," said the mother bunny.

# MY WORLD

a companion to GOODNIGHT MOON

by Margaret Wise Brown        Pictures by Clement Hurd

For John Thacher Hurd

When he comes


(He's here)

My book. Mother's book.
In my book I only look.

**The fire burns.**

**The pages turn.**

Mother's chair.
My chair.
  A low chair.
  A high chair.
  But certainly my chair.

Daddy's slippers.
My slippers.
My pajamas.
Daddy's pajamas.
Even my teddy bear
Wears pajamas.

My dog.
Daddy's dog.
Daddy's dog
Once caught a frog.

My spoon.
Daddy's spoon.
"The moon belongs
To the man in the moon."

Daddy's boy.
Mother's boy.
My boy is just a toy
Bear.

My car.
Daddy's car.

*Bang Bang Bang—My* car.

My car won't go very far.

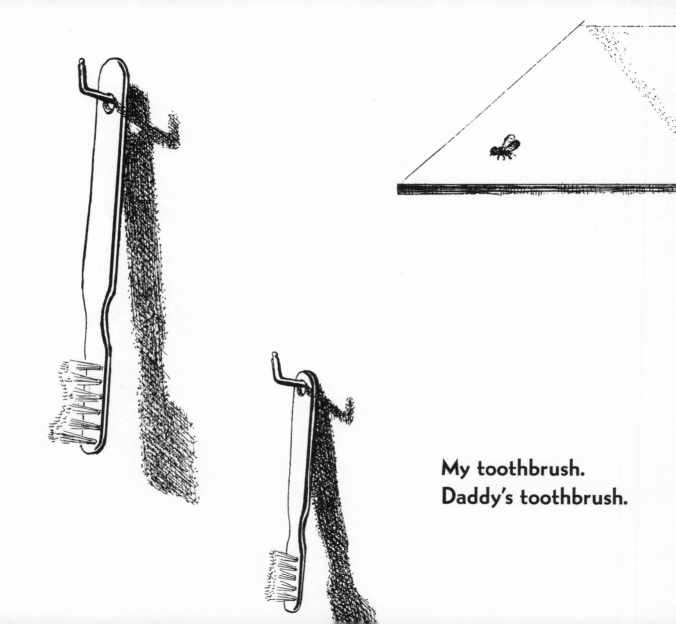

My toothbrush.
Daddy's toothbrush.

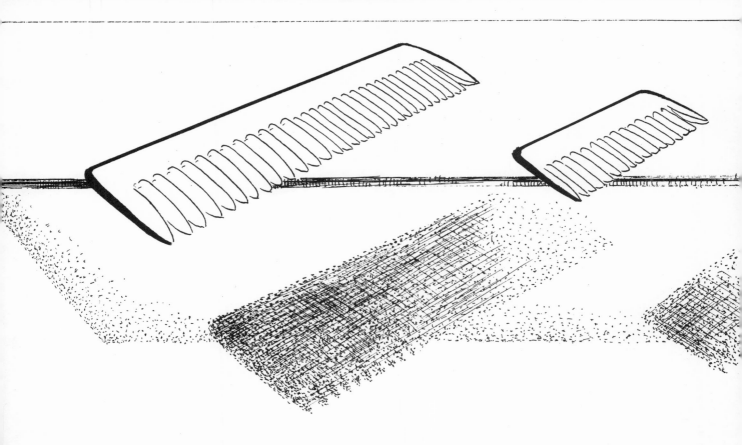

My comb.
Mother's comb.

My soap. Daddy's soap.

My soap will make soapsuds, I hope.

My fish.
Daddy's fish.
When you catch
A fish you make
A wish.

My bed.
Mother's bed.
I go to sleep
When my story is read,
When my prayers are said,
And when my head
Is sleepy on the pillow.

My breakfast.
My morning.
Daddy's breakfast.
Good morning.

My kitty.
Daddy's kitty.
Daddy's kitty
Has gone to the city.

Your world.
My world.

I can swing
Right over the world.

My tree.

The bird's tree.

How many stripes
On a bumble bee?